Praise for the Novels of Lynn Viehl

Lords of the Darkyn Novels

Nightbred

"A fast-paced, absorbing read."
— The Good, the Bad, and the Unread

"A clever story with swashbuckling adventure . . . *Nightbred* [is] a book to really savor." — *Romantic Times*

Nightborn

"Lynn Viehl is an amazing storyteller. *Nightborn* strikes through the heart with stunning strength, creating an addictive, complex world — and characters who are so alive that turning the last page will make you feel as though you're losing the best friends you wish you could have. Especially in a fight."
— *New York Times* bestselling author Marjorie M. Liu

"A clever, rip-roaring adventure from start to finish with more twists and turns than a back road in the French countryside. Loved it, loved it."
— #1 *New York Times* bestselling author Patricia Briggs

The Kyndred Novels

Dreamveil

"The Kyndred story line is fast-paced throughout, as the action never stops. Yet the cast is strong, as is the romantic triangle containing a delightful unexpected late twist. . . . This urban fantasy is pure magic." — The Best Reviews

"Followers of the series won't want to skip this one. Even though *Dreamveil* raises more questions than it answers, Rowan is a great heroine and, if you're a fan of the series, there are revelations that you won't want to miss."
— All About Romance

"Viehl's imaginative spin-off series continues as she once more explores the hazardous world of the genetically altered Kyndred. This story is rife with stunning secrets, treachery, and betrayal . . . . keep readers guessing. With . . . . tive characters, the revelations . . . . nce fans take note: This new . . . . nusual turn." — *Romantic Times*

continued . . .

Evermore

"Full of exciting twists and turns."   —*Publishers Weekly*

"Lynn Viehl sure knows how to tell a hell of a story."
—Romance Reviews Today

"Another highly satisfying chapter in the Darkyn saga."
—Vampire Genre

Night Lost

"Viehl had me hooked from the first page . . . exceptional. . . .
I definitely recommend this marvelous book."
—Romance Junkies

"Fast-paced and fully packed. You won't regret spending
time in this darkly dangerous and romantic world!"
—*Romantic Times*

Dark Need

"A must read."   —Vampire Genre

Private Demon

"Lynn Viehl's vampire saga began spectacularly in *If Angels Burn*, and this second novel in the Darkyn series justifies
the great beginning."   —Curled Up with a Good Book

If Angels Burn

"Erotic, darker than sin, and better than good chocolate."
—Holly Lisle

"This exciting vampire romance is action-packed. . . . Lynn
Viehl writes a fascinating paranormal tale."
—The Best Reviews

NIGHTBOUND

LORDS OF THE DARKYN

———

Lynn Viehl

A SIGNET SELECT BOOK

SIGNET SELECT
Published by the Penguin Group
Penguin Group (USA) Inc., 375 Hudson Street,
New York, New York 10014, USA

USA | Canada | UK | Ireland | Australia | New Zealand | India | South Africa | China

Penguin Books Ltd., Registered Offices: 80 Strand, London WC2R 0RL, England
For more information about the Penguin Group visit penguin.com

First published by Signet, an imprint of New American Library,
a division of Penguin Group (USA) Inc.

First Printing, May 2013
10 9 8 7 6 5 4 3 2 1

ISBN 978-0-451-23981-5

Printed in the United States of America

PUBLISHER'S NOTE
This is a work of fiction. Names, characters, places, and incidents either are the
product of the author's imagination or are used fictitiously, and any resemblance
to actual persons, living or dead, business establishments, events, or locales is
entirely coincidental.
  The publisher does not have any control over and does not assume any
responsibility for author or third-party Web sites or their content.